Tapenum's Day

A Wampanoag Indian Boy in Pilgrim Times

by KATE WATERS
Photographs by RUSS KENDALL

SCHOLASTIC
HARDCOVER

SCHOLASTIC INC.
New York

Kwe. Hello.

My name is Tapenum. I am Wampanoag. My people have lived on this land for all remembered time. When I was younger, strangers came from across the sea. We call them *wautaconuoag,* coat-men. They set up a colony a half day's walk from here. Now they share the land with us.

Today I start on a plan to become stronger and to improve my hunting. Even though I've promised myself before, this time I am serious. Yesterday I found out that the *pniesog* came and took away all the boys they had chosen for initiation. I was not chosen.

Pniesog are warriors and advisors to our *sachem,* our chief. They are strong, skillful, wise, and kind. They choose boys who are strong in body and spirit. My friends and I all hoped to be picked. I am disappointed. This year I have grown so tall, and I was sure they would choose me. I wonder why they didn't.

Today I will follow my plan. I will practice tracking animals; fletching my *kouhquodtash,* my arrows; shooting straight and true; and learning stillness in the forest. And I will run long distances every day.

This is our summer planting ground near Namasket, where we live until the frosts come. The soil is good, and this year our corn is growing tall. The streams and ponds are full of fish. Animals are plentiful in the forests. Wussukhumsqua, my mother, and my little sister, Numpakou, care for the corn. If they can keep blackbirds from eating it before it is ripe, we will have enough to last us all winter.

Before the sun is up, it is quiet in our *wetu,* our house.

I asked my father, Weeshatoon, to wake me early this morning so that he will know I am serious about training. My father hopes that I will become a *pniese.* It would bring great honor to our family.

breechclout and stone knife

noohkik pouch (pouch for ground parched corn)

I prepare quietly to go hunting, so I won't wake my mother and sister.

The breechclout that I tie around my waist is made of soft deerskin.

I hang my stone knife around my neck.

I check that my pouch is full of *noohkik,* ground parched corn, and I tie it around my waist.

My *petan,* my quiver, is new. I made it from the skin of a fox.

I pick up my *ahtomp,* my bow, and open the door flap to see the day.

petan (quiver)

ahtomp (bow)

As I set out for the forest, the sun is rising. It has not warmed the ground yet, and the birds are just beginning to sing. I say prayers to our Creator, Kiehtan, and to the spirits of the animals. I ask for success in hunting today. Since it is the first day of my serious training plan, I am eager to bring back a good catch to my mother.

I have had nothing to eat all morning. It is best to hunt before the first meal because hunger makes the hunter more serious. But now I grow impatient. I am too hungry to wait, so I decide to rest and have some *noohkik*. A little bit will quickly fill my stomach.

Walking through the forest, I follow the animal paths.
I look for droppings as signs that animals are nearby.
I listen and watch. Many times I turn my head just as
a rabbit disappears under the brush. At a place where
there are many of the young green plants that rabbits
like, I decide to stay still and wait. I shoot my
kouhquodtash, but I am always too early. I break one
when it hits a tree instead of a rabbit! Perhaps I should
not have eaten so soon.

I need to concentrate on hunting, but I can't stop
wondering why I wasn't chosen for initiation this year.

I put these thoughts aside. At last, I hit a rabbit and, later on, a squirrel. This is a good catch for me!

I walk quickly back to the *wetu,* thinking of hot food. My arms and shoulders ache from drawing the *ahtomp* so many times. I give my catch to my mother. She seems pleased, even though my father has returned with a turkey. I think of how much strength it takes to shoot an animal that large! If I am this tired after one morning, will I ever be that strong?

My mother gives my father a bowl of *sobaheg,* a bowl
of stew, and Numpakou and I help ourselves. Numpakou
talks on and on about her morning. "A hundred birds
came from the sky and I shouted and stomped my
feet, and sang loud songs, and scared them away from
the corn."

Later, my friend Nootimis comes by to go fishing. On the way to the pond we are quiet. We don't need to speak to know what the other is feeling. Finally Nootimis says, "I was sure you would be chosen this year, Tapenum. I'm sorry."

"The only good thing about it is that we can be together for another year," I say.

We find our *mishoon,* our canoe, and set our lines with dried clam necks for bait. The fish are quiet today, and we are only catching small ones.

23

I tell Nootimis about my training plan to hunt every morning and to take a long run in the afternoon. "I'll never keep up with you at running," he says, "but I will come hunting with you. We can practice fletching our *kouhquodtash*."

Even the small fish stop biting, so we pull the *mishoon* onto the shore. It is time for my run. I ask Nootimis to come, too. "If we practice every day, we will be strong enough to run to the colony and back. Wouldn't you like to see what the coat-men are building now?" But Nootimis shakes his head no and turns toward home.

As I start to run I see smoke in the distance. There are no planting grounds near here. *Who would be making a fire in the middle of the day?* I wonder. But I don't slow down, even though I sometimes feel brave and other times feel scared. I wish that Nootimis was with me. The smoke is closer now. At the far end of the pond I see the camp. *Could it be the coat-men?*

I try to approach quietly, like a warrior. It is an old man making a *mishoon*. I have seen him before. He is called Waban, and people say he knows all the wisdom of our ancestors. To be respectful, I am quiet until he sees me.

"*Kwe,*" Waban greets me.

"*Kwe,*" I say, and I offer him the few fish I have caught. I hope that he will let me stay with him for a while. Perhaps he will know the secrets of being chosen for initiation.

Waban sends me off to get water and more wood
for his fire. He speaks of knowing my father and my
mother. When he was younger, Waban was a powerful
pniese.

When he asks me to stay, we cook the small fish.
Then I ask him to help me practice fletching a *kouhquodt*.

He shows me how he prepares the sinew and the glue. I watch him wrap the sinew around the quill end of the feathers and the shaft. It takes him a long time to finish just one *kouhquodt*.

When it gets dark, we sit beside the water. I complain about how long it takes to prepare a *kouhquodt,* and he looks at me sternly and says, "You are impatient. Wisdom of spirit and strength of body take a long time to achieve. Every small thing you learn must be learned well. Otherwise you will have cracks like a hastily made *mishoon.* You must learn to be patient if you want to become a man."

I listen to the night sounds and understand the truth of what Waban has said. I must also practice patience. After a time we talk again. I ask about the coat-men and their visit to our place. Waban speaks of the land and the water and the many beings that inhabit them.

"There is enough for all people," he says.

I ask Waban if I can share his fire since I am so far
from home. He welcomes me and gives me a skin.
As I fall asleep, I go over the fletching in my mind.
Tomorrow I will show Nootimis what I've learned!

I look up and see shapes in the stars — Mosq, the
Bear, and the three hunters. Waban's advice echoes in
my thoughts. I say a prayer to Kiehtan and ask him to
help me learn patience and to become a *pniese*.

I am tired from hunting and fishing and thinking so
much today. The warmth of the fire puts me to sleep.

Wunniook. Be well.

More About the Wampanoag Indians

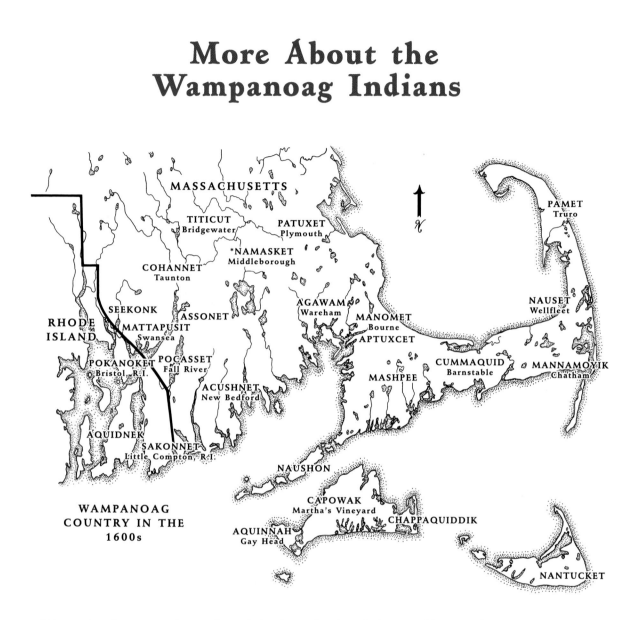

This map gives place names as they were known in the 1600s and, underneath, the names of the towns today. Tapenum lived in Namasket, which is 15 miles west of Patuxet, where the English established their colony.

How We Know About the Wampanoag People

The Wampanoag culture is a living culture. Today there are many Wampanoag people living in Massachusetts and Rhode Island.

In order to find out how the people lived during the 1620s, when the Europeans settled at Plimoth Plantation, researchers gather information through archaeological digs. Pottery, jewelry, tools, and weapons that are dug up offer clues as to how the Wampanoag lived. And stories, passed down from generation to generation, tell of heroes and gods and the history of the People.

Researchers also turn to the written records of the first European colonists. These letters, diaries, and early histories of the European communities in the New World describe the native people, the clothes they wore, the crops they planted, the food they ate, their government and social organizations, and their beliefs.

It is clear from the documents that the colonists learned little about the Wampanoag. Early colonial practical application of Wampanoag knowledge was limited to raising native crops and travel. The colonists used the Wampanoag's extensive communication network of trails and waterways and adopted the use of dugout canoes. People today have gained more practical knowledge from the Wampanoag than the early colonists did.

The Wampanoag Year

The Wampanoag people were planters as long as 1,000 years ago. In the spring, when the oak trees began to get leaves, they would leave their winter towns, and each family would move to its allotted planting ground. They grew corn, squash, beans, and other vegetables. After the harvest, they moved back to their winter towns, which were in areas that offered protection from the harsh winters. In the winter, the men hunted deer and other big animals. These animals, and a store of dried corn, were the staples of their winter diet.

This seasonal migration enabled the Wampanoag to conserve firewood, which was their essential fuel.

The Wampanoag Indian Program at Plimoth Plantation

The Wampanoag Indian Program has a homesite at Plimoth Plantation called Hobbamock's Homesite. That is where the photographs for this book were taken. It represents an unusual situation—a year-round occupation of a Wampanoag family attached to a colonial village. The staff are dedicated to sharing the Wampanoag culture with visitors. They plant and tend corn, weave mats and baskets, burn out canoes, and prepare food. The people working at the homesite do not pretend to be characters who lived in 1620, however. They talk to visitors as themselves, from their twentieth-century perspective, sharing what is known about Wampanoag life.

Becoming a *Pniese*

A *pniese* was a special kind of warrior counselor. Of course, all the men were prepared to defend their community if they were needed. But the *pniesog* were set apart by their spiritual power as well as their physical strength. The spirit beings, or *Manit*, gave these men the special powers. Boys who were chosen for initiation were taken away from their families and trained in a group. Training was very hard. Boys had to endure physical challenges and competitions, like running through thorny bushes and through a kind of gauntlet in which they were beaten on their legs. Once the strongest boys were chosen, they then had to go through a fasting ritual. They did not eat, and they drank only a special drink made of herbs that caused them to vomit. Once their bodies were cleansed, they waited reverently for the spirit being to visit them. If they had a vision, then it proved that they were destined to be *pniesog. Pniesog* were known for courage, wisdom, courteousness, humanity, and great physical strength. They advised the chief, were sent as delegates to other communities (including the new European settlements) to mediate differences, and served as examples to young children.

Glossary

English Words

Breechclout — loincloth 8

Coat-men — translation of the Wampanoag word *wautaconuoag*, used for non-Native people 2

Fletching — attaching feathers to arrows . . . 2

Quiver — a case for arrows 8

Sinew — tendon from an animal 32

Wampanoag Words

Ahtomp (ah-TOMP) — bow 8

Kouhquodt (singular) (cow-quat) — arrow 31

Kouhquodtash (plural) (cow-qua-tash) — arrows 2

Kwe (KWAY) — hello 2

Mishoon (mih-SHOON) — boat, dugout canoe 23

Noohkik (no-kick) — parched corn 8

Petan (pee-TAN) — quiver 8

Pniese (pa-NEES) — warrior counselor 7

Pniesog (plural) (pa-NEE-sog) — warrior counselors 2

Sachem (SAY-chum) — chief 2

Sobaheg (so-BAH-heg) — stew 20

Wampanoag (wam-pa-NO-og) — The People 2

Wautaconuoag (plural) (wah-ta-KON-og) — coat-men 2

Wetu (WEE-too) — house 7

Wunniook (wuh-NEE-uck) — be well 36

Wampanoag Names and Meanings

Nootimis (NOO-ta-miss) — oak 22

Numpakou (NOOM-pa-koo) — jewel or treasure 5

Tapenum (TA-pa-num) — he is sufficient . . . 2

Waban (WAY-ban) — wind 26

Weeshatoon (WEE-sha-toon) — mouth 7

Wussukhumsqua (WUH-suh-HUM-skwa) — meaning unknown 5

Who Is Issac Hendricks?

Issac Hendricks is the boy who plays Tapenum in this book. He is a Mashpee Wampanoag. Issac was chosen to be part of this book by the assistant curator of the Wampanoag Indian Program. Issac was eleven years old and in sixth grade when these photographs were taken. He plays baseball and basketball, hunts and fishes, and dreams of being a professional basketball player. He hopes to work at the homesite at the museum when he is older.

To Carolyn Freeman Travers
—K.W. and R.K.

Many thanks to the staff of the Wampanoag Indian Program at Plimoth Plantation, especially Nanepashemet, Director; David Walbridge, Site Supervisor; Linda Coombs, Assistant Curator; Darius Coombs, Assistant Site Supervisor; Toneka Pires, Foodways Supervisor; Windsong Blake, WIP Interpreter; Milton Hendricks, WIP Interpreter; and other plantation staff: James W. Baker, Chief Historian; Carolyn Freeman Travers, Director of Research; Carol City, Director of Public Relations; and Lisa Walbridge.

To the wonderful people who are the "cast": Issac Michael Hendricks, who is Tapenum; Wampsikuk Mills, who is Nootimis; Linda Coombs, who is Wussukhumsqua; Milton Hendricks, who is Weeshatoon; Cheźlyn Tiexeira, who is Numpakou; and Windsong Blake, who is Waban. And, of course, to their families for their help and moral support.

Thanks also to Aaron Hendricks for the rabbit and squirrel; and Corey Cullen, Michael Emord, James T. Freeman, and Katherine A. Freeman for the fish. To Kris Kirby, photographer's assistant, and Christian Hollyer, video assistant.

We are grateful to Dianne Hess, our editor, for seeing this book before a word was written or a picture was taken; and to Marijka Kostiw, Associate Art Director, for the design; and to Lynette Phillips, for her patient ear and wise suggestions.

Map on page 37 by Heather Saunders.

Library of Congress Cataloging-in-Publication Data

Waters, Kate. Tapenum's day: a Wampanoag Indian boy in pilgrim times / by Kate Waters; photographs by Russ Kendall.
p. cm.
ISBN 0-590-20237-5
1. Wampanoag Indians — Juvenile literature. 2. Massachusetts — History — New Plymouth, 1620–1691 — Juvenile literature. 3. Massachusetts — Social life and customs — To 1775 — Juvenile literature. 4. Pilgrims (New Plymouth Colony) — Juvenile literature. [1. Wampanoag Indians. 2. Indians of North America. 3. Pilgrims (New Plymouth Colony) 4. Massachusetts — Social life and customs — to 1775.] I. Kendall, Russ, ill. II. Title.
E99.W2W38 1995 974.4'8200973 — dc20 94-36060 CIP AC

12 11 10 9 8 7 6 5 4 3   7 8 9/9 0/0

Printed in the U.S.A.   37
First printing, May 1996
Designed by Marijka Kostiw

The photographs in this book were taken with a Nikon F4 camera on 20mm, 85mm, and 180mm Nikkor lenses. Some scenes were lit with Norman 400B portable lights. Mr. Kendall used Fujichrome 50 film.